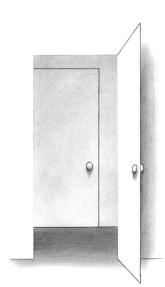

OLIVIA
saves the circus

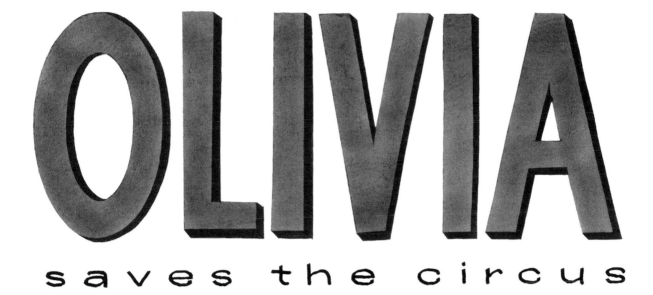

written and illustrated by Ian Falconer

An Anne Schwartz Book
ATHENEUM BOOKS FOR YOUNG READERS

New York   London   Toronto   Sydney   Singapore

Before school, Olivia likes to make pancakes for her new little brother, William, and her old little brother, Ian.

This is a big help to her mother.

After a nice breakfast, it's time to get dressed.

Olivia has to wear this really boring uniform.

Of course you can always accessorize.

Beep, beep—coming through.

Olivia

Today is Olivia's turn to tell the class about her vacation. Olivia always blossoms in front of an audience.

"One day my mother took Ian and me to the circus," she begins.
"William couldn't come because he still has to nap.

"But when we got there, all the circus people were out sick with
ear infections.

"Luckily I knew how to do everything.

"I was Olivia the Tattooed Lady. I drew
the pictures on with marker.

"Then I was Olivia the Lion Tamer

"and Olivia the Tight-rope Walker

"I was the Flying Olivia,

"and Olivia, Queen of the Trampoline,

"and I walked on stilts

and juggled

and was Olivia the Clown

and rode a unicycle.

"and for the grand finale, Madame Olivia and her Trained Dogs. They weren't very trained.

"And that's how I saved the circus.
And now I am famous.

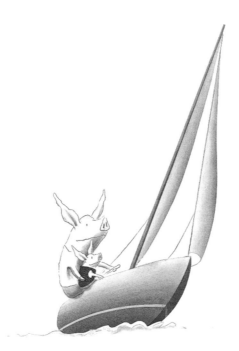

"Then one time my dad took me sailing The End."

"Was that true?" Olivia's teacher asks.

"Pretty true," says Olivia.

"All true?"

"Pretty all true."

"Are you sure, Olivia?"

"To the best of my recollection."

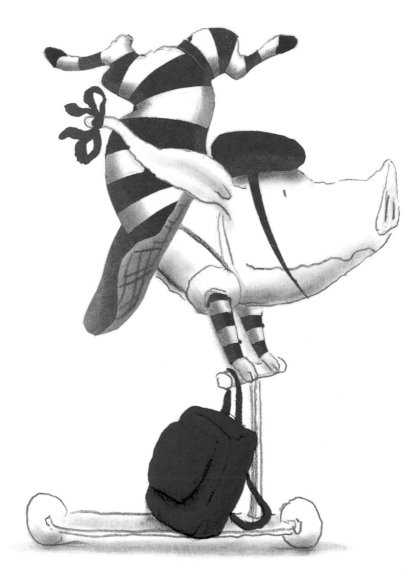

Gracefully, Olivia heads home.

"How was school today, darling?"
Olivia's mother asks as usual.
"Fine," says Olivia.
"What did you do?" asks her mother.

"Nothing."

It's bedtime, but of course Olivia's not at all sleepy.

"Good night," says her mother.

"Good night, Mommy," says Olivia.

"Close your eyes."

"They are closed."

"Then go to sleep."

"I am asleep."

"And remember, no jumping."

"Okay, Mommy."

"OLIVIA, I said, 'No jumping'!
Who do you think you are—
Queen of the Trampoline?"

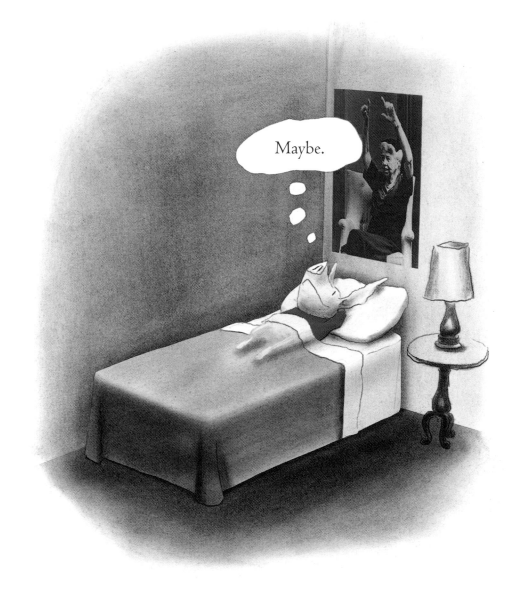

To my mother, who always, for better or for worse, encouraged me

Atheneum Books for Young Readers
An imprint of Simon & Schuster Children's Publishing Division
1230 Avenue of the Americas
New York, New York 10020
Copyright © 2001 by Ian Falconer
Book design by Ann Bobco
The text of this book is set in Centaur.
The illustrations are rendered in charcoal and gouache on paper.
The poster in Olivia's room is actually a photograph of Eleanor Roosevelt, reprinted courtesy of
the Franklin D. Roosevelt Library and Digital Archives, located in Hyde Park, New York.
Printed in the United States of America
3 4 5 6 7 8 9 10
Library of Congress Cataloging-in-Publication Data
Falconer, Ian.
Olivia saves the circus / written and illustrated by Ian Falconer.
p. cm.
"An Anne Schwartz book."
Summary: At school, Olivia tells about her summer vacation and how,
when she went to the circus and all the performers were out sick, she saved the day,
becoming Olivia the Tattooed Lady, Olivia the Lion Tamer, the Flying Olivia, and more.
ISBN 0-689-82954-X
[1. Pigs—Fiction. 2. Circus—Fiction. 3. Schools—Fiction.] I. Title.
PZ7.F1865 Om 2001
[E]—dc21
2001022676